The Three Little Pigs

Miles Kelly

Once there were **three little pigs**. They lived happily with their mother until the day came for them to make their own way in the world.

"Good-bye!"

"Bye Mum!"

"Goodbye Mum!" said the three little pigs.
"We'll call you as soon as we can."

They hadn't gone far when the three little pigs decided to stop for a picnic. "Where are we going to live?" the little girl pig asked her brothers.

Then one of the little boy pigs saw a farmer with a cartload of straw. "Perfect house-building material," said the little pig, and he bought the whole load.

The little pig soon built his straw house.
Suddenly he heard a voice outside say, "Let me
in little pig!" It was a hungry wolf.

"Not by the hair on
my chinny chin chin!"
replied the little pig.

"Then I'll huff and I'll puff and I'll BLOW your house down!"

The wolf blew down the house of straw, but the little pig managed to escape.

The two other little pigs carried on their way, until they met a woman with a huge load of sticks. The second little boy pig bought the sticks and built a house.

Then along came the big bad wolf. He knocked on the door of the stick house.

"Let me in little pig, let me in!"

But the second little pig said,

"Not by the hair on my chinny chin chin!"

"Then I'll huff and I'll puff and I'll BLOW your house down!"

As the house of sticks was blown down, sticks flew everywhere, hitting the wolf on the head.

The second little pig made his getaway. He ran off as fast he could to find his brother and sister.

Now, the little girl pig had bought a load of bricks, and set about building a strong, sturdy house.

Home sweet home!

She worked very hard, and soon the house was ready. The little pig was very pleased with herself.

The third little pig settled into her new home. But soon there was a knock at the door. It was her brothers!

Bang bang!

The boy pigs told their sister about the big bad wolf. Together they came up with a plan.

Soon there was another knock at the door. The third little pig peeked out of the window. It was the

big bad wolf.

And the wolf huffed and puffed, and puffed and huffed. But the brick house was very strong. Inside, the little pigs put a big pot of water on the fire to boil.

"You won't escape!" called the wolf, and he clambered onto the roof and began to climb down the chimney.

"Hee hee!"

But the little pigs were ready for him. The huge pot of water in the fireplace was bubbling away.

Suddenly there was a huge **SPLASH** as the wolf fell into the pot of bubbling water.

"Hurrah!" the three little pigs cheered. "The big bad wolf is dead!"

And the three little pigs lived happily ever after in the house of bricks.